S0-DMX-097

EPIC CHARACTER HANDBOOK

By Meredith Rusu

Scholastic Inc.

ISBN 978-1-338-50904-5 (Target)
ISBN 978-1-338-53885-4 (School market)

10 9 8 7 6 5 4 3 2 1   19 20 21 22 23
Printed in the U.S.A.   40

First printing 2019
Book design by Dawn Guzzo

TABLE OF CONTENTS

INTRODUCTION

Hello, and welcome to this amazing character handbook to *The LEGO® Movie 2™*! If you're reading this book, you're probably familiar with Emmet and his awesome adventure from the first LEGO movie, and now you're excited to learn who's who in the second part. Guess what? You've come to the right place! Within these pages are tons of fun facts and cool info about Emmet's best friends—and new frenemies!—from his incredible journey. And not just that, we've also added some stuff about the cool new places from this adventure!

A lot has changed in Bricksburg since Emmet's first adventure. DUPLO aliens have invaded, the city is called Apocalypseburg, and everything is decidedly *not* awesome. Then, when Lucy, Batman, Unikitty, Benny, and Metalbeard get taken by an alien commander, it's up to Emmet to save them. Along the way, he meets new allies and weird frenemies, travels to strange alien worlds, and has faith that with the power of friendship, everything can still be awesome.

So, are you ready to discover all the wacky stuff that could only happen in the second part of an epic LEGO adventure? Excellent—turn the page, and let's go!

EMMET BRICKOWSKI

Even though the city of Bricksburg is now Apocalypseburg, not much has changed about Emmet. He's still rocking his orange construction uniform and loves enjoying the awesomeness of each day. Emmet's friends tell him that he needs to act tougher since their world has been torn apart. But he's just so gosh-darned happy to be together with his best buddies, it's hard for him not to see the bright side in everything!

ALL ABOUT EMMET

- UPBEAT AND POSITIVE

- FINDS THE BRIGHT SIDE IN THINGS (EVEN IN APOCALYPSEBURG)

- LOVES OVERPRICED COFFEE FOR TWO

- SINGS ON HIS WAY TO WORK

- MAKES SURE TO TELL HIS FRIENDS THEY'RE AWESOME EVERY DAY

- MAKES SURE TO WATER HIS BEST PLANT FRIEND, PLANTY, EVERY DAY

EMMET VS. THE DUPLO ALIENS

When the DUPLO aliens first came to Bricksburg, Emmet tried to befriend them by building them a great-big welcome heart out of bricks. But the aliens were more interested in eating the welcome gift than saying "thank you." Then they started eating all the bricks in sight.

THAT HEART WAS A GIFT, NOT A SNACK!

EMMET'S ROCKET HOUSE

Pretty soon, Bricksburg was reduced to rubble and renamed Apocalypseburg. Everyone was bummed out, especially Emmet's best friend, Lucy. But Emmet wanted to show her everything could *still* be awesome. So, he built her a cute little house in the middle of the desert.

Then, Emmet's friends were taken away by a strange alien commander and whisked off into outer space. That's when he realized this was no time for shabby chic DIY décor. He added rocket boosters and blaster cannons to his house in order to make it a spaceship, and now he's ready to rescue his friends!

REX DANGERVEST

Rex Dangervest is a galaxy traveling, raptor training, archaeologist cowboy. When he's not kicking butt, building furniture, or flashing an effortlessly natural smile for photographs, you can find him roaming the universe in his high-tech spaceship, the *Rexcelsior*.

ALL ABOUT REX

- SUPER-CONFIDENT

- WEARS A HARD-CORE VEST AND CHAPS
  (THEY'RE BASICALLY LEG VESTS)

- FLIES A SPACESHIP CALLED THE *REXCELSIOR*

- HAS RAPTORS FOR CREWMATES

- ACTS LIKE HE KNOWS WHAT HE'S DOING, EVEN IF HE
  DOESN'T (THAT'S CALLED LEADERSHIP)

- BELIEVES THERE'S NO GOING BACKWARD IN LIFE.
  ONLY MOVING FORWARD, AND SOMETIMES STANDING
  STILL IN A CHILL, RELAXED WAY.

REX'S RAPTORS

Rex Dangervest has an entire crew of raptors that help him travel the galaxy.

RAPTOR FIRST OFFICER

DINO-PACK BLASTER ARRAY

COLOR-COORDINATED STRIPES

ABLE TO ACT AS A PERSONAL LANDING PAD

RETRACTABLE LEGS

CUSTOM-DESIGNED LOGO

RAPTOR GLIDER

CLAWED GRIP HOOKS

BUILT-IN DESKTOP

COFFEE HOLDER

TRENDY SPACE BRIEFCASE

RAPTOR PERSONAL ASSISTANT

REX'S COOL SHIP

The *Rexcelsior* is a kick-butt spaceship that Rex built out of spare parts. It has everything an intergalactic space cowboy could need: space cannons, a hyper-light-speed combustor, a Raptor Skate Park, jumbo viewing monitors, and even a super-rad self-destruct button (can't go on an interstellar mission without one of those).

I BUILT THE *REXCELSIOR* WITH MY OWN TWO HANDS AND SHAPED IT LIKE A GIANT FIST SO THERE'S NO MISTAKING I'M READY TO BREAK DOWN BARRIERS EVERYWHERE I GO.

SWEET MAYHEM

Sweet Mayhem is the Intergalactic Naval Commander of the Systar System. Even though she was sent to capture Lucy, Batman, Metalbeard, Unikitty, and Benny so that they could participate in a Ceremonial Ceremony at 5:15 p.m. on a distant planet, she's still pretty cool. Her fighting style is super-cute meets super-combustible, and her weapons pack a pretty punch.

ALL ABOUT SWEET MAYHEM

- HAILS FROM THE SYSTAR SYSTEM

- SECOND IN COMMAND TO QUEEN WATEVRA WA'NABI

- SELF-ASSURED AND NO-NONSENSE

- FLIES A SPACESHIP THAT SHOOTS SPARKLY AMMUNITION

- FAVORITE WEAPONS INCLUDE A STICKER BLASTER AND EXPLODING HEARTS

- LOOKS SWEET BUT IS TOUGH AS HARD CANDY

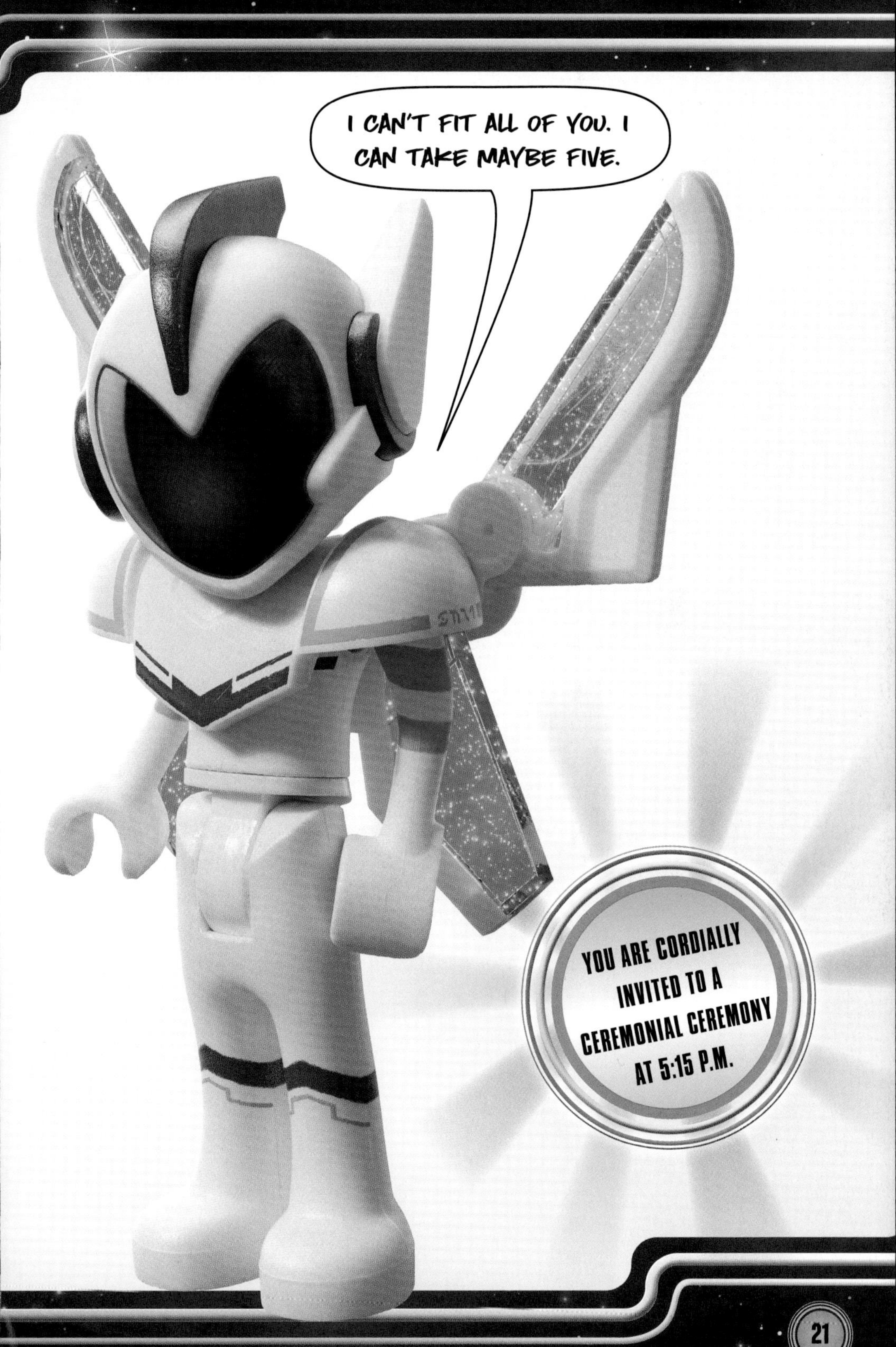
I CAN'T FIT ALL OF YOU. I CAN TAKE MAYBE FIVE.
YOU ARE CORDIALLY INVITED TO A CEREMONIAL CEREMONY AT 5:15 P.M.

SWEET MAYHEM'S SWEET GADGETS

STICKER BLASTER

This commander's weapon of choice is a sticker blaster, and anyone who goes up against it will find themselves in a sticky situation. Even Batman can't escape from its sticker sunbursts, smiley-face fruit, and silly mustaches.

LOVE YOU!

EXPLODING HEARTS AND STARS

When Sweet Mayhem needs a weapon with a little more *oomph*, she pulls out her exploding hearts and stars. These mischief makers distract their targets with cute catchphrases and terms of endearment . . . before exploding in their faces.

LOVE YOU MORE!

FORMIDABALL

Sweet Mayhem pilots the *Formidaball*, a futuristic spaceship that pumps out fresh techno beats as it scans alien planets. It also boasts an impressive arsenal of miniature exploding hearts and stars that can grow upon launch.

Though the *Formidaball* is powerful, it's not exactly roomy.

QUEEN WATEVRA WA'NABI

This shape-shifting alien queen is the ruler of the Systar System. She can morph into any shape she needs to in order to make her guests feel more at home. Queen Watevra Wa'nabi ordered Sweet Mayhem to capture Emmet's friends and bring them to a Ceremonial Ceremony at 5:15 p.m. in her recently completed space temple. She promises she's not evil. In fact, she'll give Emmet's friends everything they've ever dreamed about . . . as long as they willingly cooperate.

ALL ABOUT QUEEN WATEVRA WA'NABI

• CAN MORPH INTO ANY SHAPE SHE WANTS

• INSISTS SHE'S *TOTALLY* NOT EVIL

• LIKES SUSPICIOUSLY SECRETIVE CEREMONIES

• LOVES SINGING

• APPRECIATES THE RELAXATION BENEFITS OF A GOOD TRANQUILITY SPA.

QUEEN WATEVRA WA'NABI'S MANY *NOT* EVIL QUALITIES

- UN-DUPLICITOUS
- UN-MALICIOUS
- UN-CONNIVING
- UN-NASTY
- UN-SINISTER
- UN-NEFARIOUS
- UN-UNPLEASANT

LUCY

When the DUPLO aliens invaded Bricksburg, Lucy knew there was only one choice: fight back or go down trying. She's ultra-battle hardened now and is always on the lookout for suspicious extraterrestrial activity. When's she's not defending the city or going on recon missions, she likes to relax with deep brooding sessions overlooking the Apocalypseburg desert.

ALL ABOUT LUCY

- HAS PERFECTED THE ART OF BROODING

- LOVES COFFEE (IT'S THE BITTER LIQUID THAT KEEPS HER GOING)

- SPORTS INFRARED GOGGLES AND A WEATHERED COWL

- DOESN'T LIKE TALKING ABOUT HER BACKSTORY (SHE DOESN'T EVEN LIKE LOOKING IN THE REARVIEW MIRROR)

- EVEN THOUGH SHE'S SUPER TOUGH, SHE'S STILL EMMET'S BEST FRIEND (E&L 4-EVA!)

LUCY'S TOUGH APPROACH

Queen Watevra Wa'nabi told Lucy and the others that she would give them their hearts' desires if they went along with her ceremony, but Lucy wasn't buying it. She was the first to point out that the queen was just putting the prefix "un" in front of evil-sounding words to describe herself. And though everyone else seemed in awe of the queen's ability to grant their dreams come true, Lucy knows from experience that nothing in life is as awesome as it seems.

BATMAN

Batman is probably the only one who was just a little sad about the apocalypse. Why? Because it looks *good* on him. He's constructed a high-tech covert Citadel to protect the citizens of Apocalypseburg (he's an expert on secret fortresses, after all). And he's enhanced his wardrobe with everything from beefed-up armor and chain mail to blacker-than-black Batarangs.

ALL ABOUT BATMAN

- STILL ROCKING THE DARK AND BROODING LOOK—ONLY NOW, WITH EVEN DARKER BROODING

- KNOWS THAT BLACK AND BROWN CAMO ARE MEGA-FLATTERING ON HIM

- HITS EVERY TARGET ON THE FIRST TRY—EVERY TIME.

- PROTECTS THE CITY WITH HIS VAST ARRAY OF DEFENSE MECHANISMS—HE'S REALLY HUMBLE ABOUT IT

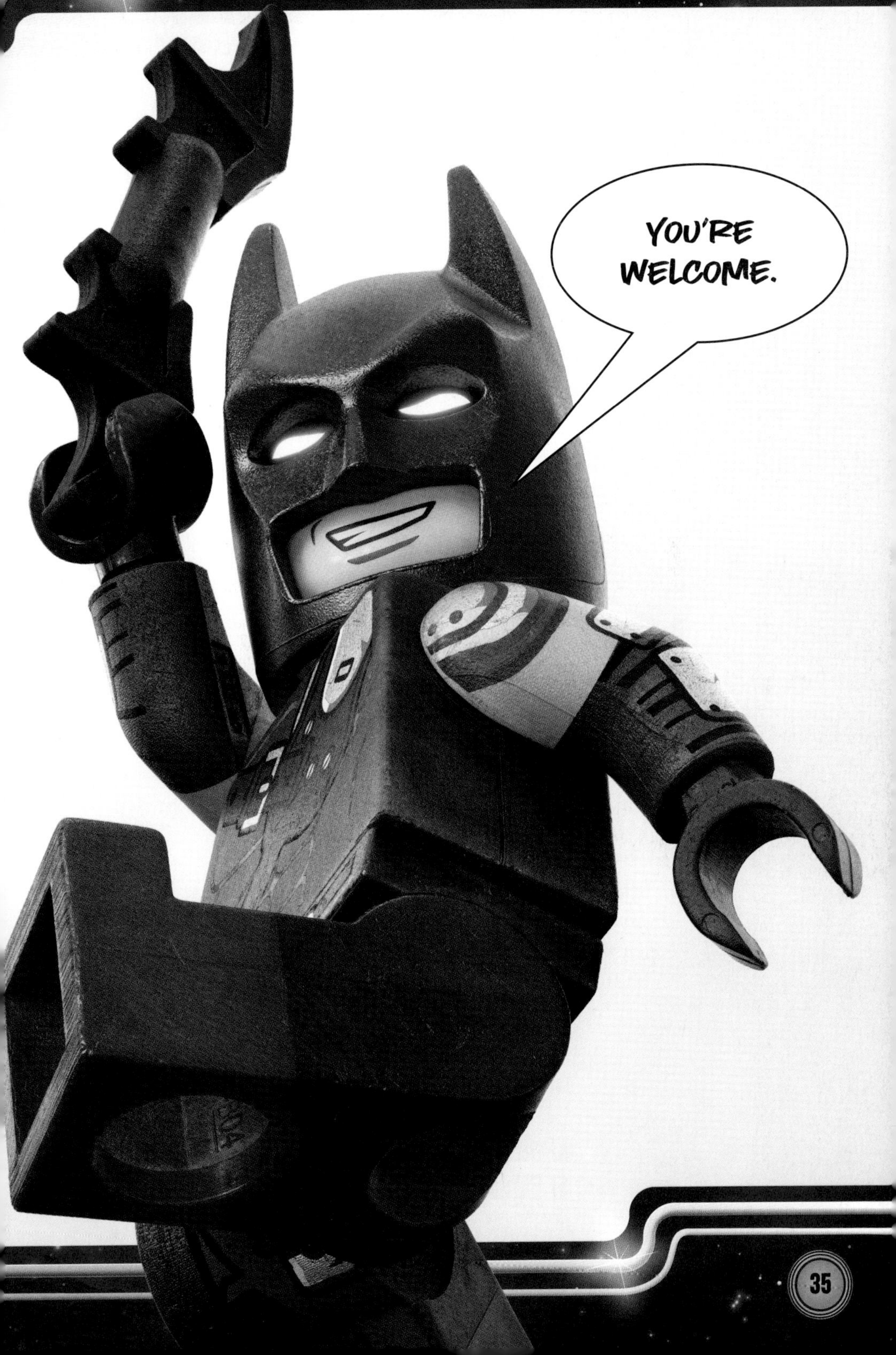
YOU'RE
WELCOME.

BATMAN'S APOCALYPSEBURG STYLE

Apocalypseburg was crying out for a leader to guide them through the end times. And Batman knew that leader was him (obviously). So it was crucial that he amp up his apocalypse style to the max. Times a billion.

FIERCE GAZE

GRITTED TEETH

INFINITE SUPPLY
OF BATARANGS

VULCANIZED RUBBER
SHOULDER PADS

RIPPED CAPE
(FOR DRAMATIC EFFECT)

#1 FAN

Queen Watevra Wa'nabi is intrigued by Batman . . . Just what she has in mind is unclear!

QUEEN WATEVS GETS ME.

METAL-PLATED
UTILITY BELT

SOUPED-UP
CLAWED-TOE BOOTS

ULTRAKATTY

Princess Unikitty used to be the picture of happiness and positivity. But when the aliens started attacking, she accessed her inner rage and behold, Ultrakatty was born! Ultrakatty is an oversized fighting machine with a battle roar that can be heard across the wasteland and armor covered in as many sharp, pointy things as possible.

ALL ABOUT ULTRAKATTY

- IS STILL SWEET PRINCESS UNIKITTY MOST TIMES

- ACCESSES HER INNER RAGE TO TRANSFORM INTO ULTRAKATTY

- WEARS BATTLE ARMOR WITH CLAWS *EVERYWHERE*

- EVEN THOUGH SHE LOOKS TOUGH, SHE'S ALWAYS THERE FOR HER FRIENDS

- SECRETLY MISSES THE WAY THINGS WERE ON HER CRAZY HOME WORLD OF CLOUD CUCKOO LAND

- WHEN QUEEN WATEVRA WA'NABI PROMISED HER AN INFINITE AMOUNT OF GLITTER, IT WAS AN OFFER SHE COULDN'T RESIST

ACCESSING INNER RAGE!!!

UNIKITTY'S TRANSFORMATION

STEP 1: START WITH ADORABLE PRINCESS UNIKITTY

ANY IDEA IS A GOOD IDEA, EXCEPT THE NOT-SO-HAPPY ONES.

STEP 2: ACCESS INNER RAGE THROUGH UNSAVORY THOUGHTS

PEOPLE WHO DON'T COVER THEIR MOUTHS WHEN THEY COUGH ARE UNSANITARY!

STEP 3: TRANSFORM

FORM OF . . . ULTRAKATTY!

METALBEARD

Metalbeard has always been a master at rebuilding his body from scrap metal. And now he has more salvaged wreckage to work with than ever. But he was still missing the one thing he lost long ago—a crew. Queen Watevra Wa'nabi offered him his own planet that was actually a pirate ship and a population that was actually his crew. That was enough to get this old sea dog on her side.

ALL ABOUT METALBEARD

- HAS THE HEAD OF A PIRATE AND THE BODY OF A MULTIPURPOSE UTILITY KNIFE

- WEARS A METAL EYE PATCH

- THE ONLY THING SHARPER THAN HIS WEAPONS ARE HIS PIRATE PUNS

- RUMOR HAS IT HE SWITCHES OUT THE ATTACHMENTS ON HIS LEGS TO MATCH HIS MOOD

- DREAMS OF HAVING HIS OWN PIRATE CREW AGAIN

YAAARRRR! QUEEN WATEVRA WA'NABI'S STORY CHECKS OUT WITH ME!

METALBEARD'S TRIKE MECH

The streets of Apocalypseburg are no place for a delicate little smart car. Enter Metalbeard's Trike Mech. This oversized clunker sports more gadgets than can be counted on one pirate hook. Even its massive front tire is powered by a bladed axle that sends alien raiders running for cover. With its grappling hooks, shark blasters, and stylish wooden steering wheel, it might just be as powerful as the Batmobile. (But don't let Batman hear you say that.)

BENNY

Even though space travel has been mostly nonexistent ever since the DUPLO alien invasion, that hasn't stopped Benny from being obsessed with spaceships. He thinks about them. Dreams about them. And builds life-sized models of them. But he wanted to keep up with the changing times like his friends, so he fashioned himself a robotic claw arm to look the apocalypse part.

ALL ABOUT BENNY

- LOVES SPACESHIPS—LIKE, SERIOUSLY LOVES THEM

- BUILDS SPACESHIPS ON THE SLY IN METALBEARD'S WORKSHOP

- MIGHT HAVE WRITTEN A SONG OR TWO ABOUT SPACESHIPS—AND WATCHES DOCUMENTARIES ABOUT THEM LATE AT NIGHT

- SPACESHIPS!

GUYS,
WE WERE
JUST IN A
SPACESHIP!

BENNY'S DREAM (OF SPACESHIPS)

Queen Watevra Wa'nabi promised Benny he could build spaceships on his very own planet with his own spaceship-building team. That was all Benny needed to hear in order to be on board and space-suited up with her story. To be honest, she had him at "spaceships."

QUEEN WATEVRA WA'NABI'S ASSISTANTS

Queen Watevra Wa'nabi's best assistants run the Shambhala Health Spa and Mindfulness Center on the Planet of Infinite Reflection. They're masters of relaxation.

BALTHAZAR

This attractive, non threatening teenage vampire is the director at the Shambhala Health Spa. He highly recommends the sparkle scrub and glitter rinse.

NAMASTE.

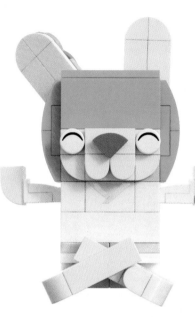

BUNNY MASSEUSE

The Bunny Masseuses at the spa know that nothing helps melt away guests' tensions like hot-stone massages.

ICE CREAM CONE

This tasty-looking treat is actually Queen Watevra Wa'nabi's right-hand man. Don't be deceived by his sweet appearance. His personality is more on the salty side.

NEW FACES, NEW PLACES!

No intergalactic adventure is complete without a ton of weird alien planets on the travel itinerary. From an apocalyptic home, sweet home and a carnivorous-plant planet to a sparkly space temple in the middle of nowhere, these locations are out of this world!

APOCALYPSEBURG

This once bright and shining city is now the desolate landscape called Apocalypseburg: a battle-hardened civilization where only the tough get by. The citizens have adapted to this new life by donning hardcore apocalyptic gear like spiked armor, welder's masks, and metal eye patches. And dark and brooding conversation is one of their favorite pastimes. But they still have an overpriced coffee shop. So, some things never change.

THE SYSTAR SYSTEM

The Systar System is made up of eleven colorful planets orbiting a sparkly blue sun. Queen Watevra Wa'nabi's palace is hidden on the sun under its brilliant atmosphere, and she rules supreme over the entire system.

PLANETS

- ROLLER VIKING PLANET
- DUPLO PLANET
- FRIENDOPOLIS/CAPITAL: HARMONY TOWN
- CUTOPOLIS
- PANTRYLIOPOLIS
- VAMPIROPOLIS
- MONOLITIOPOLIS
- ANTHROPORMORPHIA
- PLANET OF INFINITE REFLECTION
- HAWKMYNOTAURUS
- OZZIELAND
- ABSTRACTCONCEPTOLIS

THE STAIRGATE

In order to reach the Systar System, one must first pass through the Stairgate: a cosmic vortex of colors and shapes. The Stairgate is filled with asteroids and unknown dangers. Not many who traverse it return to tell the tale.

CUTOPOLIS

Cutopolis is inhabited by adorable little Plantimal aliens who love to meet—and eat—new visitors. They'll hide in the thick jungle vines and bushes, waiting to come out and chomp down on anything that moves.

HARMONY TOWN

Harmony Town is located on the planet Friendopolis, and it's a picture of perfection. The buildings are spotless. The houses match just so. Even the stars are perfectly aligned. The inhabitants keep it that way by tricking visitors into believing the town is too perfect to leave.

PLANET OF INFINITE REFLECTION

The Planet of Infinite Reflection is home to the Shambhala Health Spa and Mindfulness Center. It's where inhabitants of the Systar System go to relax, unwind, and literally lose themselves in the soothing vibes of catchy music.

SPACE TEMPLE

Queen Watevra Wa'nabi knew that for an event as special as her Ceremonial Ceremony, she would need a majestic space temple. The aliens of the Systar System have been hard at work perfecting the temple so it's ready in time for 5:15 p.m. As for what will happen at 5:15 p.m., well, only RSVP'd guests will find out.

GOOD-BYE

And that's it! You're now an expert on all the friends and places you'll encounter during a quick jaunt through the world of *The LEGO® Movie 2™*. Thanks for stopping by! And remember, keep this guide on hand in case you find yourself facing an unexpected invasion of DUPLO aliens. Or trapped on a strange planet. Or both. You never know when you'll need to count on your best buddies—and some new ones—to get out of a sticky bind. Until then, keep it awesome, and catch you on the flip!

DON'T MISS THESE  ADVENTURES!